The Usborne Christmas Magic Painting Book

Fiona Watt

Dip the brush into some water, then carefully brush it across the patterns and lines within the shapes surrounded by thick black lines. The paint will magically appear.

Try painting me!

Before you start to paint each new shape, dip the brush into water. Use the tip to fill in small shapes and the side to fill larger ones.

To stop the water from seeping through to the next page, unfold the flap at the back of the book and place it under the page you're about to paint.

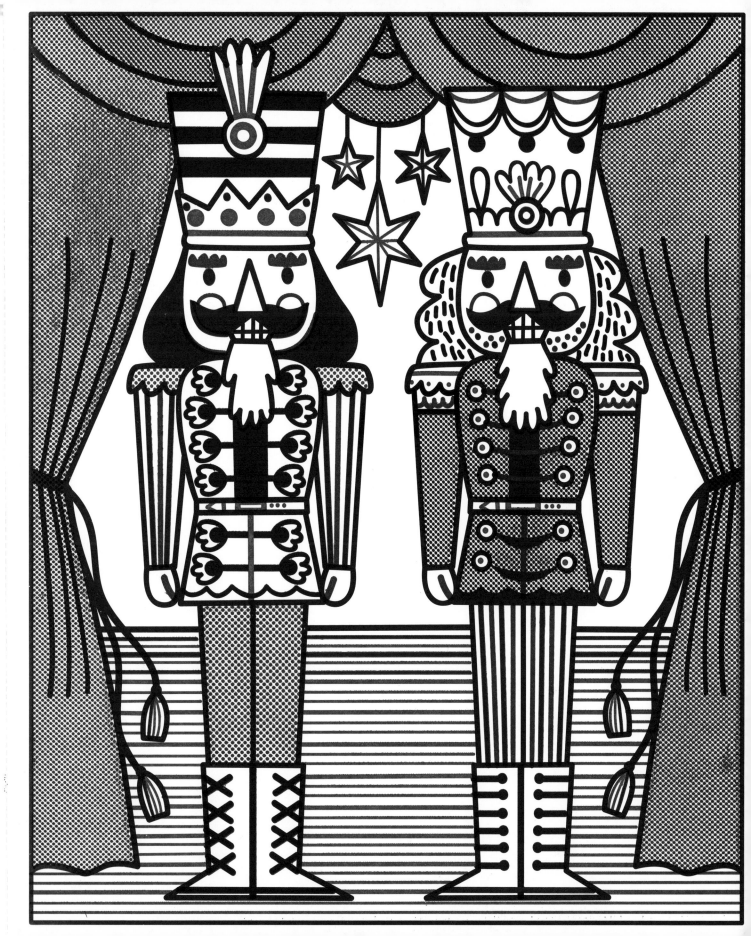